T0407180

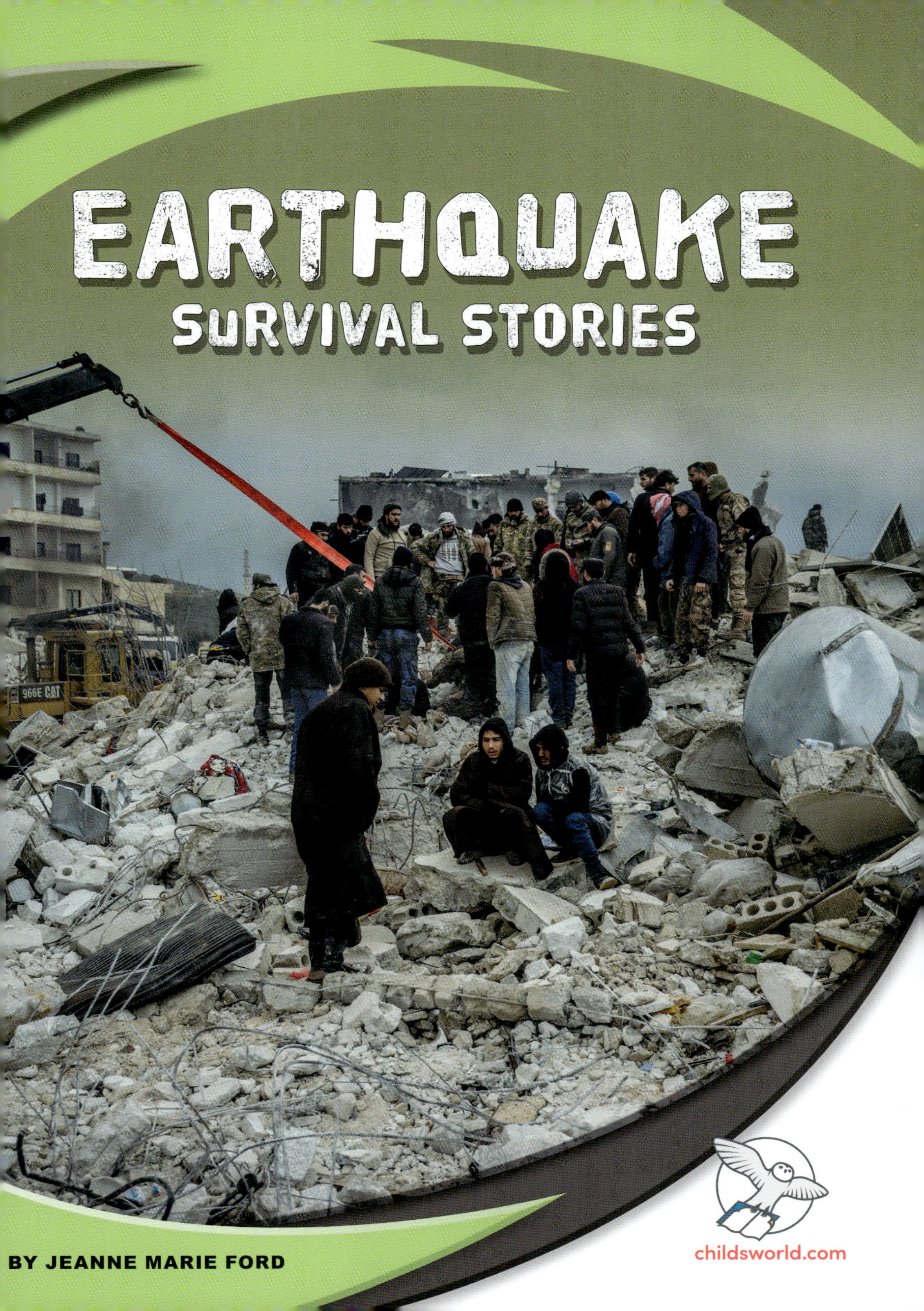
EARTHQUAKE
SURVIVAL STORIES
BY JEANNE MARIE FORD
childsworld.com

Published by The Child's World®
800-599-READ • www.childsworld.com

Photography Credits
Photographs ©: Anas Alkharboutli/picture-alliance/dpa/AP Images, cover, 1; Shutterstock Images, 5, 10, 12, 13, 16; William J. Smith/AP Images, 6; AP Images, 9; Hiro Komae/AP Images, 14; Ryu Seungil/iStockphoto, 17, 19; Parikh Mahendra N./Shutterstock Images, 20; Crystal Eye Studio/Shutterstock Images, 22; Freelance Journalist/Shutterstock Images, 24; Peter Hermes Furian/Shutterstock Images, 25; Jasminko Ibrakovic/Shutterstock Images, 26; Red Line Editorial, 28 (Antarctica), 28–29

ISBN Information
9781503854574 (Reinforced Library Binding)
9781503854840 (Portable Document Format)
9781503855229 (Online Multi-user eBook)
9781503855601 (Electronic Publication)

LCCN 2023937306

Printed in the United States of America

ABOUT THE AUTHOR

Jeanne Marie Ford is an Emmy-winning TV scriptwriter who holds an MFA in writing for children from Vermont College. She has written numerous children's books and articles, and she also teaches college English. She lives in Maryland with her husband and two children.

CONTENTS

WHAT IS AN EARTHQUAKE?

Earth's crust is divided into **tectonic plates**. These fit together like pieces of a puzzle. They move and hit against each other. The stress from this movement may release a lot of energy and cause the ground to shake. This is known as an earthquake.

Earthquakes happen every day around the world. Many are too small to be felt. They may happen deep beneath Earth's surface. They may occur in the middle of the ocean.

Sometimes the shaking produced from a large earthquake can be felt far from its **epicenter**. Smaller quakes called foreshocks may signal that a larger earthquake is coming. People may also feel **aftershocks** after the main quake.

The amount of damage from an earthquake depends on the quake's size, depth, and location. Large earthquakes that happen near Earth's surface and around large cities can cause a lot of damage. Buildings may be destroyed, and people may die.

FAST FACTS

- On May 22, 1960, there was a 9.5 **magnitude** earthquake near Chile. It caused 1,655 deaths and 3,000 injuries.
- Port-au-Prince, Haiti, experienced a 7.0 magnitude earthquake on January 12, 2010. Around 316,000 people died.
- A 9.0 magnitude earthquake stuck near Japan on March 11, 2011. The earthquake caused a **tsunami**, and the combined natural disasters left 20,319 people dead.
- On April 25, 2015, Gorkha, Nepal, experienced a 7.8 magnitude earthquake. The area was hit with an aftershock on May 12. Around 9,000 people died and 22,000 were injured.
- Two earthquakes hit Turkey on February 6, 2023, resulting in numerous aftershocks. More than 50,000 people died.

CHAPTER ONE

THE BIG ONE

May 22, 1960, was an ordinary day for eight-year-old Sergio Barrientos. He was walking near his home in southern Chile. Suddenly, he felt the ground shake beneath his feet. Wires on nearby telephone poles began to sway. They swung harder and harder. They started to hit wires on the other side of the street. Then Sergio saw chimneys crumbling off houses. The earthquake knocked Sergio to the ground. He lay there for ten minutes until the trembling finally stopped.

Later, Sergio learned that he'd lived through the strongest earthquake ever recorded. The Great Chilean Earthquake measured at least 9.5 on the Richter scale. Huge cracks opened in the streets of Valdivia, Chile. Buildings tumbled to the ground. The earthquake was so strong that it moved the coast of Chile to the west by 30 feet (9 m).

◄ **Around two million people were left homeless after the 1960 earthquake in Chile.**

THE RICHTER SCALE

The Richter scale is used to measure the size of earthquakes.

8

Earthquakes that are 8.0 or greater can demolish communities.

7

Earthquakes that measure between 7 and 7.9 are major earthquakes. They leave behind serious damage.

6

Earthquakes between 6.1 and 6.9 are considered strong earthquakes. They may leave behind major damage in cities.

5

Earthquakes between 5.5 and 6.0 are known as moderate earthquakes. They damage buildings slightly.

4

3

People can feel earthquakes that measure between 2.5 and 5.4, but these quakes don't leave behind much damage.

2

People cannot feel earthquakes that measure 2.5 or less.

▲ **The earthquake happened just off the Chilean coast, near the city Valdivia.**

The shocks from the earthquake caused volcanoes to erupt in other parts of Chile. The shocks also lifted the ocean's floor and sent giant waves rolling across the Pacific Ocean. Within a day, two tsunamis formed. One crashed into Hawaii. The other hit Japan.

Scientific instruments across the globe recorded the giant earthquake's vibrations. **Seismologists** learned many new things about Earth's structure from the quake's effects. Sergio grew up to study earthquakes, too. As an adult, he got a job at the University of Chile in the National Seismological Center.

CHAPTER TWO

BURIED ALIVE

Falone Maxi lived in Haiti and had always dreamed of becoming a nurse. But she ended up going to business school instead. On January 12, 2010, 23-year-old Maxi was sitting in class in Port-au-Prince, Haiti, when the building started to shake.

◄ **The Haiti earthquake destroyed many buildings, leaving more than 1.5 million people homeless.**

Maxi and her classmates raced from the room. As Maxi ran, one of her sandals slipped from her foot. Dust filled the air. In the stairwell, a cement block crashed down and knocked Maxi onto her back. Then another student, Mica Joseph, slammed into her. Both women lay pinned together under heavy **debris**.

Joseph had a broken leg. Maxi's head was bleeding. Her cell phone didn't have a signal. She shone its light on Joseph and saw that the woman's face was covered with bruises and cuts. Every so often, aftershocks sent more concrete raining down on the two of them. Rats scurried through the building. Maxi and Joseph took turns yelling, "We're alive." But no one came.

Soon Maxi's phone died, and the women were plunged into darkness. Maxi ripped paper from her notebook and shoved it into her nose to block the smell of death surrounding her. Her throat was dry, and her body begged for water.

Maxi refused to give up hope. She thought of all the things she still wanted to do. She would love to see the blue-green waters of the Caribbean again. Maxi wanted to play Wii tennis, and she wanted to dance.

Six days after the earthquake struck Haiti, rescue workers pulled Maxi and Joseph from the rubble. Maxi gulped in fresh air.

▲ **Approximately three million people were impacted by Haiti's 2010 earthquake.**

She felt someone pour cold water down her throat. A crowd waited outside, and Maxi saw her half-sister, Carline Joaceus. Joaceus had stood outside of the destroyed university for days. She had watched rescue workers sift through the rubble and desperately hoped Maxi would come out alive.

As Maxi was taken to a hospital, she viewed the damage from the earthquake. Buildings were gone. She saw people sleeping on streets everywhere she looked. The earthquake had only lasted 35 seconds. The Haitian government said the quake killed 316,000 people.

Doctors released Maxi from the hospital after four days. But her home was gone. Her family slept under bedsheets draped like a tent. Maxi's mother made her a bed in the dirt beside their chickens. Maxi found that she preferred to sleep under the stars. Whenever she went inside a building, she felt as if the walls were closing in on her. Maxi lived in fear of another earthquake. But she promised herself that one day she would follow her dream of becoming a nurse. She would help others as they had helped her.

TECTONIC PLATES

Earth's crust has many tectonic plates. Earthquakes happen at the places where the plates meet.

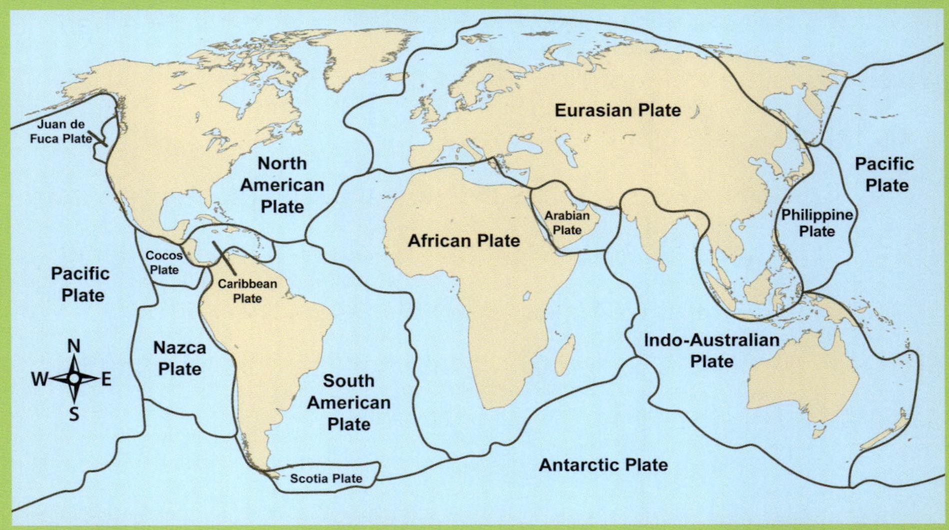

ALOKA
南相馬市
市長
桜井勝延

CHAPTER THREE

EARTHQUAKE AND TSUNAMI

Katsunobu Sakurai was the mayor of a seaside city named Minamisoma in Japan. On the morning of March 11, 2011, he attended a local school graduation. Then he went to a meeting at city hall. At 2:46 p.m., the ground began to tremble.

At first, the shaking was gentle. Then it grew stronger and more violent. People around Sakurai cried for help as cracks formed in the building's walls. Sakurai had trouble staying on his feet. He caught a water jug as it fell from his desk. He was surprised at how calm he felt.

Five or six minutes passed before the shaking stopped. Sakurai gathered people in the building. He brought them outside since aftershocks might send city hall tumbling down. He kept thinking about whether the earthquake would cause a tsunami along the coast. He thought the area around city hall would be safe.

◄ **Katsunobu Sakurai visited an evacuation center after an earthquake struck his city.**

It was 7 miles (11 km) from the ocean. But others in the city of more than 70,000 people could be in danger.

Sakurai put together a disaster response team. The members gathered outside and shivered in the cold spring air. They tried to call friends and family, but the cell phone network was down. Tears streamed down people's faces.

HOW A TSUNAMI FORMS FROM AN EARTHQUAKE

If a large earthquake happens near the seafloor, the seafloor may fall or rise suddenly. This sets off a tsunami.

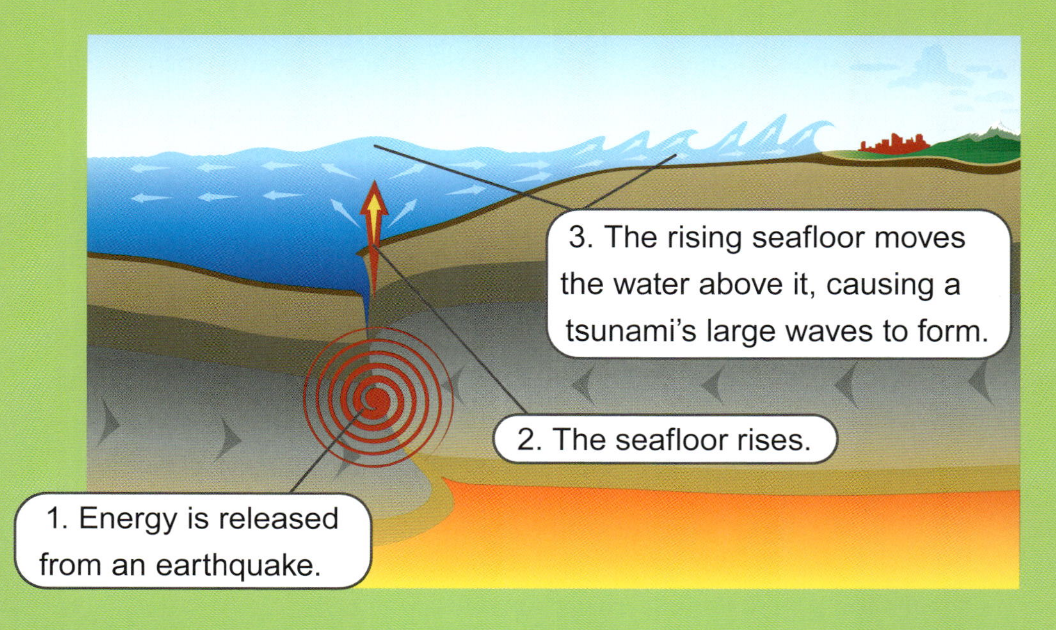

3. The rising seafloor moves the water above it, causing a tsunami's large waves to form.
2. The seafloor rises.
1. Energy is released from an earthquake.

▲ **Rescuers worked tirelessly to save people from the earthquake's destruction.**

Forty minutes later, a tsunami hit the shore. The massive wave damaged Fukushima Daiichi, a nearby nuclear power plant. The tsunami caused a power outage at the plant, leading to explosions that sent dangerous **radiation** into the air.

That night, Sakurai saw the bodies of children who had died in the earthquake and tsunami. He wondered whether any of them had been at the graduation he'd celebrated earlier in the day. The days that followed the earthquake brought little relief. The government told people near the nuclear plant to stay indoors.

Nearly everyone who could move to a safer place did. But Sakurai could not leave. His job as mayor was to take care of those left behind. About 1,500 people were dead or missing. By April, fewer than 10,000 people remained in the city.

Sakurai couldn't bring himself to look out of his office window at the glittery sea that had drowned hundreds of his people. He feared things would only get worse, and he was right. His city was running out of food and gasoline. Doctors were leaving for safer areas. More people would die if he didn't do something.

Sakurai thought of himself as someone who was "strong in the rain," in the words of his favorite poem. Now, he was desperate. Sakurai took out a small camera and began recording a plea for help. After he posted the video to YouTube, supplies began pouring in from around the world. In the end, thanks to his leadership, his city survived.

The 2011 earthquake near Japan was one of the ▶ most powerful quakes in recorded history.

CHAPTER FOUR

A SECOND CHANCE

Ten-year-old Maya Gurung lived in a small village in Gorkha, Nepal. Three times a day, she traveled up a nearby mountain to get clean water for her family. She helped her mother with cooking and taking care of the house. Maya also collected wood for cooking fires.

◄ After Nepal's earthquake, members of the army rushed to help the injured. The quake and aftershocks impacted eight million people.

April 25, 2015, was a Saturday. Since Maya didn't have school, she went into the field with her uncle and cousin to take care of the cattle. It was almost noon when the ground began to move. Rocks started rolling down from the hills above them. An earthquake had caused a landslide.

The uncle grabbed Maya and her cousin. He tried to find somewhere safe from the rocks speeding down the hill. But a boulder crashed into them. Maya's leg was severely broken from the impact, and she yelled in pain.

Maya's father was working in the fields when the earthquake hit. He saw that the homes around him had been flattened. He searched desperately for his daughter. When he finally found Maya, he took her to a clinic. The people there couldn't do much. They tied Maya's leg in rags even though her injury was serious. Maya needed more help than they could give.

A day later, a government helicopter came to take Maya to a hospital in the capital city, Kathmandu. Maya's father got on the helicopter with her. But when the helicopter stopped and more injured people were loaded on, he was forced to get off.

He was so worried about Maya that he was awake all night. The next morning, he decided that he had to go find her.

He walked and sometimes got rides as he headed toward Kathmandu. The city had millions of people. He had no idea where to start looking for his daughter.

Four days later, he finally found her. A green blanket covered Maya's legs. Tears dripped from her eyes. She held tight to her father. Doctors and nurses took pictures of their emotional reunion. Then Maya's father realized part of her leg was covered in a thick bandage. The bottom part of Maya's leg was gone. The surgeons had needed to remove it because it was so badly damaged.

EARTHQUAKES AND LANDSLIDES

A landslide is when a large number of rocks or debris start sliding down a hill. Earthquakes can trigger landslides.

1. An earthquake may put stress on a slope, loosening rocks.
2. A landslide quickly moves downhill and can travel miles from where it started.
3. A landslide may uproot trees, move rocks, and pick up or destroy anything in its path.

In that moment, Maya's father knew that her hard life would become much harder. She could no longer climb the steep paths near their house to get water. Until Maya could get a **prosthetic** leg, her father would have to carry her everywhere. She would also have trouble getting the medical care she needed in their village.

Maya stayed in the hospital for more than a week. When it was time to go home, Maya's father picked her up from the hospital bed. He put her on his back and began walking to their village.

On the afternoon of May 12, another earthquake struck Nepal. Maya and her father had just reached the town of Rumchet. While stopped there, they met a man who was raising money to help educate Nepalese children like Maya. He had a friend who was a doctor. He offered to take Maya back to Kathmandu to get the doctor's help.

Maya's father made the hard decision to leave his daughter with a stranger. Back in Kathmandu, the doctor gave Maya a prosthetic leg. In time, she learned to walk again. She started school in Kathmandu. Life would be hard, but now Maya had a chance for a bright future.

CHAPTER FIVE

A NEW LIFE

On January 27, 2023, Necla Camuz gave birth to her second son. She named him Yagiz, which means "brave one" in Turkish. Camuz and her newborn baby went home to Samandag, Turkey, where she lived on the second floor of an apartment building.

◄ **People comforted each other after the Turkey earthquake. The quake and aftershocks destroyed or damaged more than 160,000 buildings.**

An earthquake hit Turkey in the early morning on February 6. Camuz was feeding Yagiz. She tried to reach her husband and three-year-old son in the next room. But the shaking from the earthquake got worse. A wall crashed down. When the violent trembling stopped, Camuz realized she and the baby had fallen through the floor. Next to them was a toppled cabinet. It held up a big piece of concrete. The cabinet was the only thing stopping the concrete from crushing Camuz and her baby.

TURKEY EARTHQUAKES

On February 6, 2023, two earthquakes hit Turkey and impacted both that country and neighboring Syria.

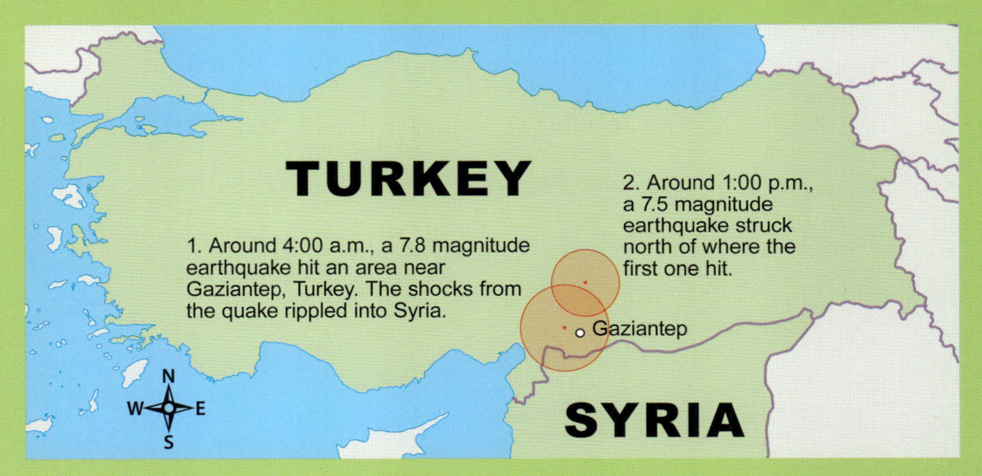

TURKEY
1. Around 4:00 a.m., a 7.8 magnitude earthquake hit an area near Gaziantep, Turkey. The shocks from the quake rippled into Syria.
2. Around 1:00 p.m., a 7.5 magnitude earthquake struck north of where the first one hit.
Gaziantep
SYRIA
N
W
E
S

▲ **Rescue dogs can smell people buried under rubble. When they find someone, they bark and scratch the ground.**

Darkness surrounded them. The dust made it hard to breathe. When she heard voices in the distance, Camuz shouted for help. She picked up some rubble and hit it against the cabinet. No one heard.

Camuz worried they would never be rescued. She wondered whether the rest of her family had survived. She told herself to be strong for her baby. She breastfed him as they lay there, even though she had nothing to eat or drink. She even tried to drink her own milk, but she couldn't.

When Camuz finally heard rescue dogs barking, she thought she might be dreaming. The rescuers asked her to knock if she was okay. Then they dug through the rubble to find her. Their flashlight pierced through the darkness. They asked how old the baby was, but Camuz didn't know. She had no idea how long they had been trapped. Later, she learned it had been four days.

At the hospital, Camuz was overjoyed to hear that her husband and older son had been saved. One day after their rescue, Camuz and her baby left the hospital. Their home was now a tent where 13 family members lived. All of them had lost their homes to the earthquake. But they were glad to be alive. Camuz said Yagiz gave her the strength to live. She was grateful he was too young to remember the quake. And she prayed he would never experience anything like it again in his lifetime.

THINK ABOUT IT

- Why do you think people live in areas with a high risk of earthquakes?
- What are some ways to help people who have lost their homes to earthquakes?
- What do you think can be done to prevent or reduce damage and deaths from earthquakes?

EARTHQUAKE MAP

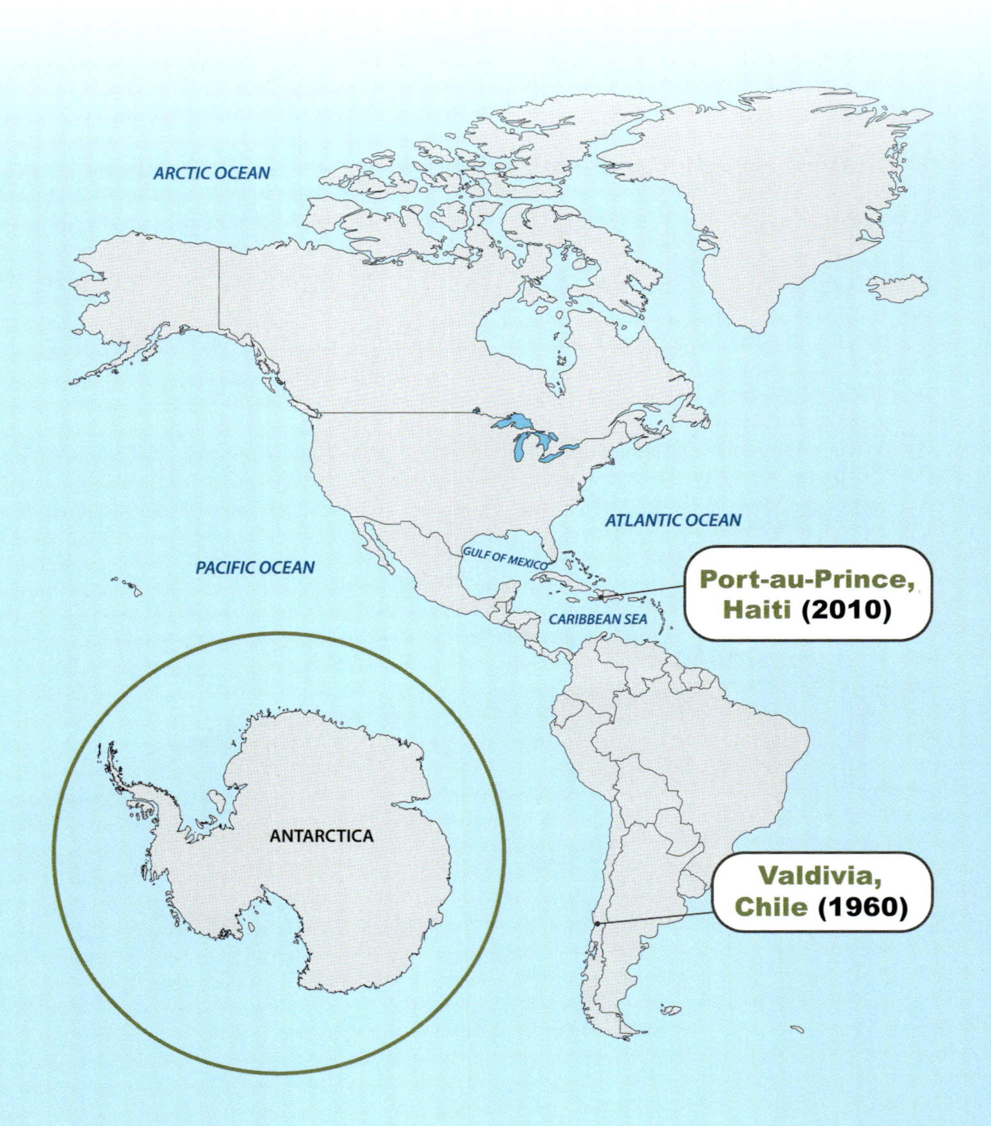

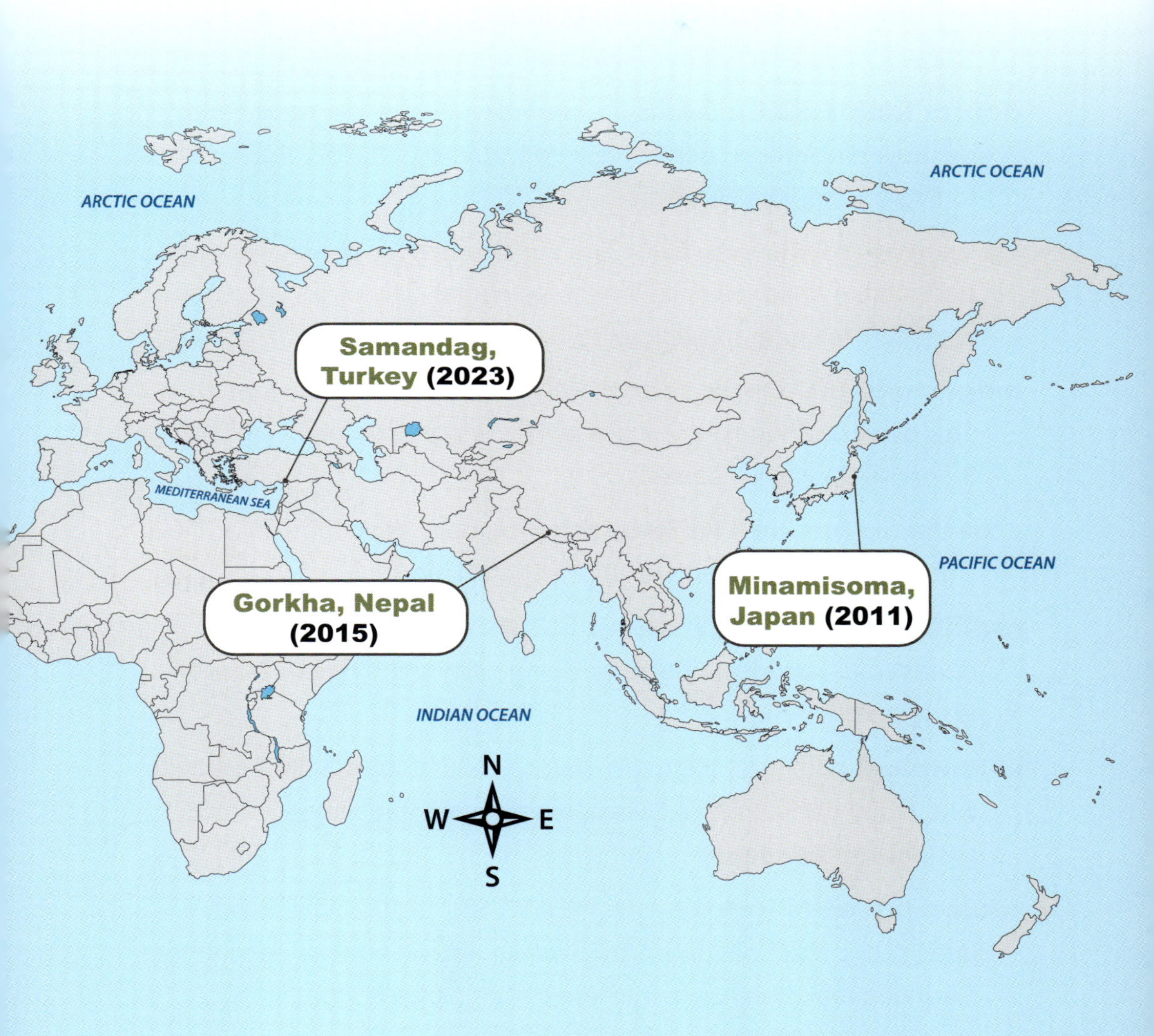
ARCTIC OCEAN
ARCTIC OCEAN
Samandag, Turkey (2023)
MEDITERRANEAN SEA
Gorkha, Nepal (2015)
Minamisoma, Japan (2011)
PACIFIC OCEAN
INDIAN OCEAN
N
W
E
S

GLOSSARY

aftershocks (AF-tur-shoks): Aftershocks are smaller quakes that follow a main earthquake. Aftershocks can cause major damage.

debris (duh-BREE): Debris are pieces of things that have been destroyed or broken down. Rescue workers removed heavy debris to find earthquake survivors.

epicenter (EP-ih-sen-tur): The surface directly above where an earthquake happens is called the epicenter. The strongest shaking is usually felt near the epicenter.

magnitude (MAG-nih-tood): Magnitude refers to the strength and size of an earthquake. The greater the magnitude of an earthquake, the more damage it causes.

prosthetic (prahs-THEH-tuhk): Prosthetic describes an artificial limb. The girl was fitted with a prosthetic limb.

radiation (ray-dee-AY-shun): Radiation is energy that is released as a wave or particle. Being around too much radiation is dangerous.

seismologists (syz-MOL-uh-jists): Seismologists are scientists who study earthquakes. Seismologists work to develop warning systems for earthquakes and tsunamis.

tectonic plates (tek-TA-nik PLAYTS): Tectonic plates are large rocks that float on Earth's mantle and hit against each other. Earthquakes often happen where tectonic plates meet.

tsunami (tsu-NAH-mee): A tsunami is a massive wave caused by an earthquake. The tsunami hit a coastal city and destroyed it.

SELECTED BIBLIOGRAPHY

Bichell, Rae Ellen. "When the Biggest Earthquake Ever Recorded Hit Chile, It Rocked the World." *NPR*, 29 Aug. 2016, npr.org. Accessed 6 Mar. 2023.

"Earthquakes." *Woods Hole Oceanographic Institution*, n.d., whoi.edu. Accessed 6 Mar. 2023.

Wald, Lisa. "The Science of Earthquakes." *USGS*, n.d., usgs.gov. Accessed 6 Mar. 2023.

FIND OUT MORE

BOOKS

Romero, Libby. *All about Earthquakes.* New York, NY: Children's Press, 2021.

Rose, Simon. *Earthquake Readiness.* New York, NY: Crabtree Publishing, 2019.

Van Rose, Susanna. *Volcano & Earthquake.* New York, NY: DK Publishing, 2022.

WEBSITES

Visit our website for links about earthquakes:
childsworld.com/links

Note to Parents, Caregivers, Teachers, and Librarians: We routinely verify our Web links to make sure they are safe and active sites. So encourage your readers to check them out!

INDEX